HUB. DUBI

THE TREE HOUSE

CHILDREN'S SIGN BOOK

Volume 2

Sebastian Metz & Lena Dietz

HUBI DUBI Children's Sign Book Volume 2

The Tree House

Sebastian Metz / Lena Dietz

Monsheimerstraße 62

67549 Worms

Mail: sebame0104@gmail.com

1st Edition

Independently Published

© 2023 Sebastian Metz

Copywriting: Sebastian Metz / Lena Dietz

Signs: Lena Dietz / Nora Edeler / Silke Fischer

Editing and proofreading: Lilith Koenen

Setting and layout: Sebastian Metz

Cover design: Farbenspiel Illustration & Design

Graphics: Farbenspiel Illustration & Design

ISBN Print: 9798856883359

Table of contents

Foreword

Dear Readers,

we are delighted to present this read-aloud book with signs of the American Sign Language (ASL). Signs are a wonderful way to expand and enrich our communication. This book uses signs of the American Sign Language to expand, and support spoken language. ASL-supported text offers a variety of benefits for both children and adults:

- **Improved communication:** ASL-supported text enables children to simultaneously use verbal and nonverbal language. This allows them to express their needs, feelings, and thoughts better.

- **Better comprehension:** ASL-supported text helps children better understand what is being said as they receive visual and auditory cues. This can significantly benefit children with hearing impairments or speech and communication disorders.

- **Promoting language development:** ASL-supported text can support children's language development by helping them better understand and use words and phrases.

- **Reducing frustration:** Children with difficulty speaking or understanding speech are often discouraged. Signing that supports spoken language can help reduce frustration by offering children another way to express themselves and be understood.

- **Inclusion:** ASL-supported text can help better integrate hearing-impaired people as well as people with speech and communication disorders into society by allowing them to participate in conversations and interactions actively.

Foreword

Overall, speech-assisted signing can be valuable to children's and adults' language development and social inclusion.

This read-aloud book tells an exciting story about deep friendship. There are up to four ASL signs on each page. A special education teacher selected the signs to help children better understand the stories and relate to the action.

The following children are the target audience for Hubi Dubi Sign Books:

- **Children with hearing impairment**

- **Children with cognitive impairment (especially trisomy 21)**

- **Children with language development disorders**

- **Children with a high urge to move**

- **Children without impairment who like to try new things**

This read-aloud book will not only bring joy to children with hearing impairments but it will give all children and adults a new perspective on the importance of signs in our society. Let's work together to ensure that sign language plays an even more significant role in our society and that we all benefit from the diversity of our communication.

We wish you much fun reading aloud and exploring.

Sebastian & Lena

Sign overview

Legend

•   Do not move

→   Direction of movement

⇒   Pulsating movement

→| Movement until stop

⇝   Repeated back and forth movement

⟷   Repeating tremor movement

Finger game

✕   Execution with touch

↔   Rotate around its own axis

→←   Merge

←→   Spread out

   Movement with opening hand

   Movement with closing hand

     Starting position of the hand

Note: All gestures are described for right-handers. Left-handers must use the left hand as the dominant hand to sign.

Sign overview

adventure

Both hands are held in front of the body at stomach level. The left hand is open and the fingers touch. The back of the hand points upward. The right hand is clenched into a fist and the index finger is extended forward. The right hand is held under the left and does not touch it. Now the right-hand pulses three times to the left. The left-hand does not move.

big
(high)

The right hand is held in front of the body at stomach level with the back of the hand facing forward. The hand is clenched into a fist and the index and middle fingers are extended. The index and middle fingers touch. Now the hand is brought straight up and stops at head level.

big
(wide)

Both hands are held in front of the body at chest level. The hands are open, and the fingers do not touch. The palms face each other, and the fingertips point forward. Now the hands are brought outward in a small arc.

bird

The right hand is held in front of the body at chin level. The hand is clenched into a fist and the index finger and thumb are extended. The thumb and index finger of the right hand are close together. The right hand is brought between the nose and mouth with the back of the hand. There the thumb and index finger touch each other twice in quick succession.

Sign overview

**blanket
(to cover)**

Both hands are held in front of the body at stomach level. The fingers are extended and bend at a 90° angle. The thumbs touch the index fingers. The fingertips point toward each other. Now the hands are simultaneously brought forward in an upward arc, touching the body above the chest.

**cold
(frosty)**

Both hands are held in front of the body at chest level. The hands are clenched into a fist. In quick movements, the hands are moved to the right and left. The elbows do not move.

dark

Both hands are held in front of the body at shoulder level. The hands are open and the fingers are touching. The fingertips point upward and the backs of the hands point forward. Now the hands are brought down to the center of the body in an arc. The movement ends when the right hand is held in front of the left chest and the left hand in front of the right chest. The palm of the right hand is to the left of the back of the left hand.

done

Both hands are held in front of the body at shoulder level. The hands are open and the fingers do not touch. The backs of the hands point forward. Now both hands are opened outward so that the palms face forward. The hands are at chest height to the right and left of the body at the end of the movement.

Sign overview

exciting
(with excitement)

Both hands are held in front of the body at chest level. The hand is open, and the fingers do not touch. The middle finger is tilted forward. The palms face the body. Both hands perform asynchronous small circular movements outward. The hands remain in front of the chest. At the same time, the head is slightly bent to the right and left.

feather
(bird)

Both hands are held in front of the body at chest level. The hands are clenched into a fist, and the index fingers and thumbs are extended. Thumb and index finger are close together at the beginning. The fingertips point towards each other and the back of the hand to the front. Now the right hand is moved diagonally upwards to the right in wave-like movements. The thumb and index finger first move away from each other and are then close together again.

floor

Both hands are held in front of the body at chest level. The fingers are extended and bend at a 90° angle. The fingertips point forward. At the beginning of the movement, the hands touch in front of the body. Then the hands are moved about 10 cm horizontally outward.

friend

The right hand is held in front of the body at shoulder level. The index and middle fingers are extended and do not touch. The other fingers are curved. The index and middle fingers point upward. The back of the hand points forward. Now the hand is moved forward a few centimeters. The middle finger is placed over the index finger.

Sign overview

friendly

Both hands are held in front of the body at shoulder level. The hands are open and the fingers do not touch. The backs of the hands point forward. The hands tilt slightly inward. The elbows remain in position. While the fingers alternately move slightly forward and backward, the hands are guided upward outward.

great

Both hands are held at head level to the right and left of the body. The hands are open and the fingers do not touch. The palms face forward. Now pulse the hands forward twice at the same time.

house

Both hands are held in front of the body at chest level. The hands are open and the fingers are touching. The thumbs are folded in. The hands form a roof with the edges of the hands on the index finger. Then the hands are moved outward and finally downward to represent the walls of the house.

Hubi Dubi

The right hand is held in front of the body at chin level. The hand is clenched into a fist and the index finger is extended. The finger is held against the lower lip and brought down a few centimeters in a pulsating motion.

Sign overview

idea

The right hand is held at head height to the right of the body. The hand is clenched into a fist and the little finger is extended. The little finger touches the right temple. The back of the hand points forward. Now the hand moves in a straight motion away from the temple.

lake

The right hand is held at chin level to the right of the mouth. The little finger and thumb touch and the other fingers are extended. The index, ring and middle fingers touch the right cheek. Now both hands are brought to chest level. At the same time, the hands are clenched into a fist and the thumb and index finger are extended slightly curved. Together, the hands are now moved further down to hip level.

outside

Both hands are held in front of the body at chest level. The left hand is open and the fingers do not touch. The fingertips point to the right and the back of the hand to the front. The fingers of the right hand are extended and bend at a 90° angle. The thumb and index finger are close together. The fingertips point downward and the back of the hand is held against the palm of the left hand. Now the right hand moves upward twice and the thumb and index finger touch each other.

perfect
(very good)

Both hands are held in front of the body at chest level. The hands are open and the fingers touch each other. The index finger and thumb touch at the fingertips. Thumb and index finger of both hands point to each other. Now both arms above the elbows move simultaneously first a little toward the body and then forward away from the body.

Sign overview

rain

Both hands are held in front of the body at head level. The hands are open and the fingers do not touch. The palms point downward. Now the hands are moved up and down several times in parallel. The elbows do not move.

roof

Both hands are held in front of the body at chest level. The hands are open and the fingers are touching. The thumbs are folded in. The fingertips touch and form a roof. Now both arms move simultaneously diagonally downward outward.

sad

Both hands are held in front of the body at chin level. The hands are open and the fingers do not touch. The fingertips point upward and the backs of the hands point forward. Now both hands are brought down a few centimeters at the same time.

sky

Both hands are held in front of the forehead at head level. The hands are open and the fingers do not touch. The fingertips point upward and the palms face forward. Now the hands are brought in an arc to the right and left of the body.

Sign overview

sun

The right hand is held at head height to the right of the body. The thumb touches the other fingers. Now the hand rotates outward once in a semicircular motion before the fingertips move toward the head and the hand opens. At the end of the movement, the fingertips no longer touch.

swan

The right hand is held in front of the body at chin level. The back of the left arm joins the right elbow at a 90° angle. The right hand is clenched into a fist and the thumb, index and middle fingers are extended forward and touching. The hand pulses forward twice. The right elbow and left arm do not move.

thank you

The right hand is held in front of the body at chin level. The hand is open and the fingers touch each other. The movement begins with the fingertips touching the chin. Now the hand is moved forward. The elbow does not move.

to fly
(bird flies)

Both hands are held in front of the body at shoulder level. The hands are open and the fingers do not touch. The palms face forward and the fingertips point upward. The hands move synchronously on the spot in up and down movements. The arms below the wrists do not move.

Sign overview

**to help
(I help you)**

Both hands are held in front of the body at chest level on the left. The right hand is clenched into a fist and the thumb is extended upward. The palm of the left hand points upward. The right hand is placed on top of the left hand. Then both hands move simultaneously in an arc to the right.

to hop

Both hands are held in front of the body at stomach level. The right hand is clenched into a fist. The index and middle fingers are extended. The left hand is open and the fingers are touching. The fingertips of the left hand point to the right and the back of the hand points downward. The index and middle fingers of the right hand touch the palm of the left hand with the fingertips. Now the right hand moves quickly upward. The fingers are curved in the process. Then the fingers of the right hand move back to the left palm.

to see

The right hand is held in front of the body at eye level. The hand is clenched into a fist and the index and middle fingers are extended. The fingertips point toward the eyes. Now the hand is brought forward horizontally a few centimeters.

to sit

Both hands are held in front of the body at chest level. The hands are clenched into a fist and the index and middle fingers are extended. The fingertips of the left-hand point to the right. The fingertips of the right-hand point forward. The backs of the hands point upward. Now the index and middle fingers of the right hand are held a few inches above the left index and middle fingers. Then the fingers of the right hand are placed on the fingers of the left.

Sign overview

to sleep

The right hand is held in front of the body at head level. The hand is open and the fingers do not touch. Now the hand is brought under the chin. At the same time the hand closes into a fist.

to swim
(breaststroke)

Both hands are held in front of the body at chest level. The hands are open and the fingers are touching. The palms point downward. Now the hands are moved in circular motions. The right hand rotates circularly to the right and the left hand rotates circularly to the left.

to walk
(run)

Both hands are held in front of the body at chest level. The hands are open and the fingers are touching. The fingertips point downward and the backs of the hands point forward. Now the hands are alternately lifted outward to the front several times. The arm below the wrists does not move.

tree

The right hand is held right at head level in front of the body. The top of the left arm joins the right elbow at a 90° angle. The right hand is open, and the fingers do not touch. Now the hand is rotated back and forth.

Sign overview

wall

Both hands are held in front of the body at chest level. The hands are open and the fingers are touching. The thumbs are folded in. Now both hands are held in front of the body at shoulder height. The palms face forward and the hands touch at the outer edges of the index fingers. Now both hands are moved outward simultaneously to shoulder width.

warm

The right hand is held in front of the body at chin level. The fingers are extended and bend at a 90° angle. The thumb touches the other fingers. The fingertips touch the chin and the back of the hand points forward. Now the hand moves forward a few centimeters. As it does so, the fingers open so that the hand is open at the end.

weather

Both hands are held in front of the body at shoulder level. The hands are open and the fingers do not touch. The palms face forward. Now the hands move downward in small wave-like movements. The right hand starts with a wave to the right, the left hand with a wave to the left.

wet

Both hands are held in front of the body at chest level. The fingers are extended and bend at a 90° angle. The thumb and index finger are close together. The fingertips point upward and the backs of the hands face forward. Now the thumb and index finger touch each other 2 times in quick succession. The wrists do not move.

Sign overview

wood

Both hands are held in front of the body at chest level. The hands are open and the fingers are touching. The fingertips of the left hand point to the right and the back of the hand points upward. The right hand rests with the outer edge of the little finger on the back of the left hand. The fingertips point forward. Now the right hand moves forward and backward several times on the left hand.

HUBI DUBI

THE TREE HOUSE

Hubi Dubi

Who is Hubi Dubi?

Hubi is Birdie's best friend. He lives in the forest.
He shares his inspiring adventures with you every day.
Every evening you will hear one of his new stories
and fall asleep with great excitement.

Hubi Dubi   friend   adventure

The robin "Birdie"

Who is Birdie?

Birdie is Hubi Dubi's best friend.
Birdie is a little robin and lives in the little forest, too.
His home is the big tree right by the lake.
Birdie and Hubi have many adventures together.

bird   big (high)   tree   lake

The swan

Who is the swan?

The majestic swan is a grumpy contemporary.
His home is the big lake.
There, he proudly swims back and forth all day.
You can always rely on the swan.
He is always polite and friendly. But it is best not to annoy him.

| swan | lake | to swim | friendly |

The little forest

"Hubi Dubi, Hubi Dubi, open the door quickly.
It's so **wet** and stormy **outside**."
Birdie stands in despair in front of Hubi Dubi's **house**.
It's raining cats and dogs in the woods.
The robin can't even fly properly anymore.
His **feathers** are soaking wet and heavy from the **rain**.

wet   outside   house

24

feather   rain

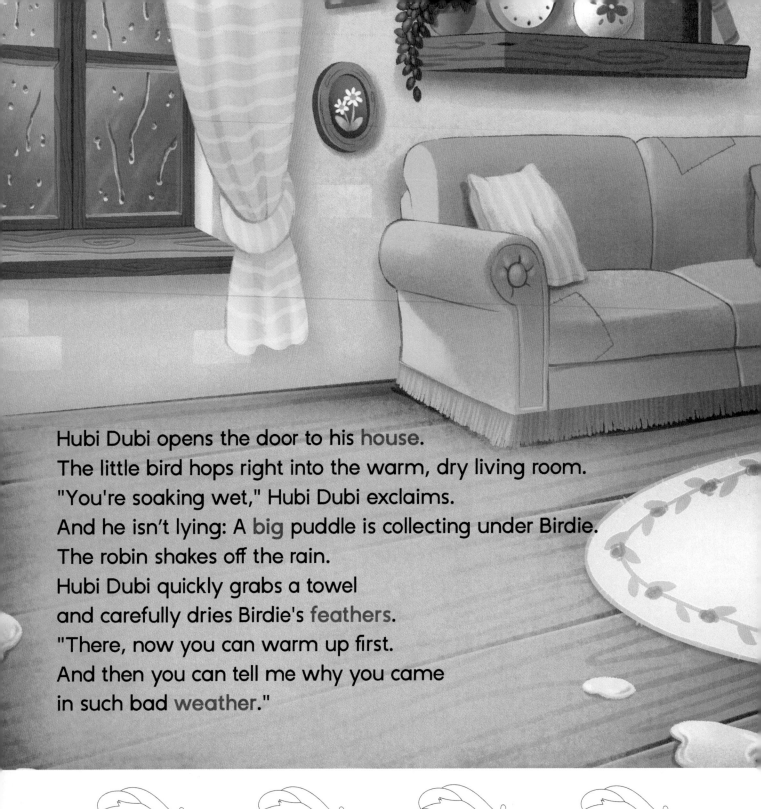

Hubi Dubi opens the door to his house.
The little bird hops right into the warm, dry living room.
"You're soaking wet," Hubi Dubi exclaims.
And he isn't lying: A big puddle is collecting under Birdie.
The robin shakes off the rain.
Hubi Dubi quickly grabs a towel
and carefully dries Birdie's feathers.
"There, now you can warm up first.
And then you can tell me why you came
in such bad weather."

| house | big (wide) | feather | weather |

"Oh, Hubi, it's always so nice and **warm** and dry at your place. It's always wet and **cold** on my tree by the lake when it rains," chirps the little bird with **sadness**, his head hanging low. What could possibly **help** the little bird?

warm   cold   sad   to help

"I have an idea, Birdie, we'll build you a tree house!
Then you'll have a dry and warm home."
Birdie is irritated.
"A tree house? A house in my tree? Is that possible?"
"Of course!" exclaims Hubi Dubi with excitement.
Birdie is thrilled and jumps up in the air with joy.
The two go down to the cellar.
"Let's think. What do we need to build a tree house?" ponders Hubi.
"We definitely need wood," says Birdie.
"That's right," nods Hubi Dubi, "and tools.
We need a big saw and a hammer and lots of nails.
"Hubi Dubi and Birdie pack up all their things
and walk together to the big tree by the lake.

idea   tree   house

exciting

wood

to walk

Meanwhile, the rain in the forest has stopped
and the first rays of sunshine are shining through the trees.
Sweating, Hubi Dubi and Birdie reach the tree.
They lay the tools and boards on the ground.
"First we build the base plate.
You can sit, walk and sleep on it," Hubi Dubi suggests.
Hubi climbs up into the tree with the boards
and begins to nail them together.
The robin flies Hubi up the nails piece by piece.

sun   to sit   to walk   to sleep

Hubi Dubi quickly finishes the floor slab.
"It already looks really good, Hubi," chirps Birdie happily.
"Thank you. Now we'll build the walls."
Birdie flies the nails up again.
Hubi nails one board after the other all around.
These are the walls.

floor   thank you   wall

"And now the most important thing,"
says Hubi Dubi, "The roof, so that it doesn't rain in!"
Hubi takes the big boards and puts them on top.
"They are perfect for the roof."
One last time, Birdie flies the nails to Hubi.
Hubi hammers the boards together to form a sturdy roof.

roof   perfect   to fly

"Done!" Hubi calls out. "The tree house is ready!"
"Wow, that's great. A real house in my tree,"
the robin is happy and immediately hops in with Hubi.
"Look, Birdie, you can see the lake through the window.
And you can see my house, too," Hubi exclaims enthusiastically.

| done | great | to hop | to see |

sky   dark   tree

No sooner are the two finished, than the sky closes in.
It gets darker and darker.
After a short time, a blanket of clouds covers the entire forest.
Splash. The first drop falls on the tree house, then a second.
And suddenly it rains in torrents.
But that doesn't bother Birdie and Hubi Dubi.
The two are sitting warm and dry in Birdie's tree house.
"Hooray!" shouts the robin. "We have built a great tree house!
Thank you Hubi. It's a great new home"
"My pleasure, Birdie."

house

rain

warm

"Birdie, I can't go home now. If I leave now, I'll get all wet. Can I sleep with you tonight?"
"Of course! That would be nice," chirps the little bird,
"Here's a warm blanket for you."

wet   to sleep   warm   blanket

A book for all children?

Did you like the story of Hubi Dubi and Birdie?

Or do you have suggestions on how we can improve our book?

Creating this book was a heartfelt endeavor for us and we spent a lot of time and effort completing it. That's why we would love it if you would leave us an honest review on Amazon. It's the best way for us to tailor this and future books to your needs and continue to support your children in their language development through play.

Your Opinion Matters

Did we get you excited about ASL?

Our signs are based on the sources listed below. You can use the links to teach yourself and your children more signs. Because of the different dialects, there are often several signs for one word. That's why a sign shown in our book does not always correspond to the sign available in the online sources. We have tried to keep the signs in our Hubi Dubi Children's Sign Book as simple as possible.

Sources:

- https://www.spreadthesign.com/de.de/search/
- https://www.signingsavvy.com/

Author descriptions

Sebastian Metz

Sebastian is an April fool of the Generation Y. With his easy, structured and pragmatic nature, he quickly wins people over with his ever-emerging ideas.

After his high school graduation In the Nibelungen city of Worms, he first started his business studies without much orientation. What started as an escape plan developed into an A-level master's degree.

Nowadays, Sebastian is a full-time consultant for banks and financial service providers. This is not a job where he can fully live out his creativity. Thus, he came up with the idea of writing children's books as a side hustle. For Sebastian, the idea of "Hubi Dubi" is not just any children's book, but has emotional value, too. After all, his father came up with all of the stories for him when he was still a little boy himself. What Sebastian's father recorded 25 years ago on a children's tape recorder is now written down in this book for the first time. His aim: the stories should not collect dust in the attic, rather they should live on in the hearts of many children.

Author descriptions

Lena Dietz (affectionate special needs educator)

Lena is the pedagogical and emotional element of Sebastian's work. With her cheerful, positive and carefree nature, she quickly wins over the hearts of those around her.

As early as her elementary school days, Lena's Diddle friend book read: I want to work with children. Even in her youth, she discovered through her part-time jobs and her days with the Boy Scouts that working with children and young people gave her great joy. Today, she's turning her wish into reality at Heidelberg University of Education: Lena is a future teacher for children with a concentration in mental development.

Lena was thrilled by Sebastian's idea for a children's book from the very beginning. During an internship at a special needs school for children specializing in mental development, she came up with the idea of adding sign language assistance to the children's book. After all, many of her students use signs to communicate more effectively. But she couldn't find any exciting children's books in which German Sign Language signs were taught in a playful way. This is how the idea for the Hubi Dubi children's sign books came about. Lena's greatest wish is to teach new ways of communication to as many children as possible and to give children without disabilities access to signs. That's why she decided to publish the "Hubi Dubi Children's Sign Books" also on the English market.

Made in the USA
Monee, IL
11 November 2024

69852135R00024